HENRY'S BOOTS

Henry's feet began to tingle. At first he thought it was just because he wasn't used to wearing boots, but it wasn't really that kind of tingle.

As the game got underway Henry's toes began to twitch. His feet started to throb and the tingle got much stronger and rose up through his body. It was the same surge of power that he'd felt when he had first put on the boots, but this time it was much stronger.

Meanwhile, in front of him Henry's team mates were ignoring him as they always did.

"Over here ... to me..."

Maybe they thought those thunderbolt shots were just lucky strikes...

"Here! Over here!"

...but things were about to change!

Other Hippo Sport titles:

The Winning Touch
David Hill

Hopeless Haynes and the No-Hopers
Martin Hodgson

Football Mad
Paul Stewart

HIPPO SPORT

HENRY'S BOOTS

Antony Lishak

To
W:4
[signature] Antony L...

Hippo

To Debs,
my tactical supremo
midfield dynamo
and all round superstar
with love.

Scholastic Children's Books
Commonwealth House, 1-19 New Oxford Street,
London WC1A 1NU, UK
A division of Scholastic Ltd
London ~ New York ~ Toronto ~ Sydney ~ Auckland

First published in the UK by Scholastic Ltd, 1988

Text copyright © Antony Lishak, 1998
Inside illustrations copyright © Harry Vening, 1998

ISBN: 0 590 19807 6

Typeset by TW Typesetting, Midsomer Norton, Somerset
Printed by Cox & Wyman Ltd., Reading, Berks.

10 9 8 7 6

CHAPTER 1

Henry loved football. His bedroom was papered with posters of players. He collected stickers, badges, programmes and pennants. He drank from a football mug, slept under a football duvet, washed himself with football soap and slept in football pyjamas. His dreams were filled with winning goals and laps of honour. He was a fanatic.

But there was one problem. Although he could name every post-war captain of

England, reel off the nicknames of every British club from the Toffees to the Magpies and fully understand the off-side rule ... as a footballer, he was useless! At least that's what everyone else thought. But Henry was sure that hidden inside his fragile frame was a superstar waiting to emerge like a butterfly out of its cocoon.

For the moment Henry remained a footballing caterpillar – although it wasn't for lack of practice. After school each day he would wolf down his tea, change into his kit and dash into the garden. He would practise shooting, passing, heading, dribbling and trapping until it was too dark to see ... or he'd lost the ball. (Henry held the world record for asking the next-door neighbour to return his ball. One day he had to ask for it sixteen times – in the end the ball was returned in two halves!)

Henry had broken more windows, trampled on more shrubs and ruined more grass than any other young footballer. If the England manager chose his players by how well they fell flat on their faces then Henry would be a superstar one day! If the right way to kick a ball was to slice it in a totally unpredictable direction, then there would be a best-selling video called "Football – Henry's Way"! In short, to the outside world, Henry knew as much about how to play football as an elephant knows about flying!

This apparent staggering lack of skill did not dent Henry's grand ambitions, however. He desperately wanted to play for his school team. At the end of each Tuesday training session he would go up to Mr Grace, the teacher in charge, and ask if he would be picked. "Maybe next time" was the closest he ever got to a "yes".

But Henry was a determined boy. After each rejection he would go home, scoff a few biscuits and go into the garden for a quick slice-about before bed time.

At first Henry's parents tried hard to understand their son's obsession. His dad used to spend every free moment playing football in the garden with him. But he soon abandoned all hope of becoming a superstar's father. Initially his mother saw no harm in him spending all his pocket money on football magazines. "At least he's reading something!" she would say. But gradually their patience wore thin. They could no longer put up with the awful bath-time chanting. They were fed up with being woken by screams of joy as Henry scored another goal in his dreams. But worst of all was the running commentary Henry gave on practically everything he did. Only yesterday his mother had heard from the bathroom:

"...and with breath-taking skill Henry Davis pulls the chain and manages to pull up his trousers before the water stops flushing! Quite amazing!"

They decided to tackle the problem head on...

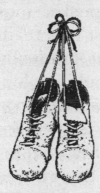

CHAPTER 2

"Come inside, Henry!" called his mother through the kitchen window. "Your supper's ready. It's your favourite, spaghetti Bolognese."

The back door flew open and there stood Henry.

"Don't forget to take your trainers off, there's a good lad," she said. "And do be careful not to rub against the wall."

Henry's mother used to be a mild-natured woman, but in recent months she had felt her tolerance levels dropping rapidly.

"Now, love, what do you want to drink?"

 "Henry Davis enters the room. Mud-stained after another long and gruelling training session, he deftly moves towards the table. Barely taking his eye off the target he swerves past the fridge, avoids a dangerously high tackle from the washing-machine door and lands perfectly on the chair. As the kitchen echoes to the chant of 'HENRY! HENRY!' he coolly leans forward and asks his mum for a glass of milk."

"Here you are." Henry's mother handed him his drink and sat down opposite her son. "Only about two weeks to go now!" she said, trying to stay calm.

Henry forced a pile of spaghetti into his mouth and sucked hard to ensnare the final few strands.

 "Henry Davis, eleven in fifteen day's time, swiftly wipes the sauce from his

chin. Then, with a magician's sleight of hand, he skilfully twirls his fork and aims the ball of spaghetti straight at his open mouth!"

"Your father and I have decided to get you a really special birthday present. It's something that will help you stay fit and give you the chance to get out and about a bit more. A racing bike!"

Henry put down his fork. He said nothing.

"We've seen just the one!" continued his mother, her voice charged with forced enthusiasm. "It's red with special alloy wheels. Ten gears, speedometer, drinking bottle…"

"Henry Davis slowly sips his drink…"

He slowly sipped his drink.

 "Then, sick as a parrot, he pushes the remains of his once tasty meal away…"

Henry pushed his plate to the middle of the table.

"Regaining his composure, as only he can do, he stands..."

Henry stood up...

"But Mum, you said I could have a pair of football boots!"

"Your father and I think that maybe you should start to think of some other pastime..."

"Pastime!" Henry yelled, abandoning his commentary. "Football is my future! It is my career, my destiny, my entire life! How can you do this? I need a pair of boots! To deny them would be like gagging a young singer, handcuffing a promising pianist, blindfolding a budding painter! How could you do this? Who needs wheels! I've got legs, haven't I?"

"Henry, calm down," his mother said. "You're acting like a baby."

"Well, maybe that's because I'm being treated like one!" Henry grappled with his shirt, pulled it hard over his head and threw it venomously to the ground. Then he charged towards the door.

 "Henry Davis, the usually mild, self-controlled soon-to-be eleven-year-old, turns and leaves the field of play in disgust!"

Henry went upstairs for an "early bath".

9

CHAPTER 3

"Good morning, Henry. And what would you like for breakfast?"

Henry's father was a big man. He could easily have been mistaken for a weight-lifter or body-builder. His neck was at war with his shirt collar and his buttons were on the verge of popping. His closely shaved head and stubbled jaw added to his "don't-mess-with-me" look. But seldom have appearances been more deceptive. Jeff Davis was a mild-mannered accountant who rarely raised his voice, a gentle giant who would do almost anything to avoid confrontation. His general approach to life was to lead it as quietly as possible. He had heard about his son's out-burst the previous night and decided to go in to work late, intent on smoothing things over.

"Toast? Cereal? Tea?" he enquired. "Maybe an egg or two?"

Henry sat down at the table and reached out towards the toast rack.

"Jam? Marmalade? Or just butter?"

"Stop faffing about, Jeffrey!" said Henry's mother from another room. "Let him stew in his own juice!" Clearly she was still smarting from last night's argument.

Henry noticed his football shirt on the floor exactly where he had thrown it. He prepared himself for a tough breakfast.

Henry's father poured some tea and slid it across the table towards his son. "I understand you had a little run-in with your mother last night," he whispered. "Don't fret, lad. It'll soon blow over!"

"She said I couldn't have boots for my birthday," said Henry. "That I should think of taking up an other pastime. As if football was just a phase I was going through! You know how important it is to me."

"Yes, well, you see..." Henry's father often started sentences like that. "...oh, never mind!" And ended them like that.

Mrs Davis came into the kitchen. She stood over the football shirt, hands on hips. "And what do you intend to do about this, Henry Davis?"

Henry stood up and took a deep breath.

"Under immense pressure Henry Davis swoops down low, grabs his shirt, sends his mother the wrong way and fires it straight into the washing-machine... GOAL!"

Henry slammed the washing-machine door shut.

"Very good. Yes. Very funny, Henry," said his father, trying desperately to relieve the tension. "Now come and finish your toast."

"Don't encourage him, Jeffrey. The lad has to be told."

"Told what?" asked Henry.

"Go on, then, 'man-of-the-house', tell him!" Henry's mother sat at the table between her husband and her son. She leant back in her chair and folded her arms, waiting.

"You see – well… It's like this. We thought that maybe it would be better if, all things taken into consideration, you thought long and hard about … well … about your … er…"

Henry's mother could wait no longer. She decided to drop the bomb herself. "Henry Davis, face the facts. You are just no good at football. You have never been any good and you show no signs of ever improving. Accept it. You may love the game but you just can't play it. You should stop going to football training and wasting your time."

Henry suffered the pain of hearing all this in silence. He had always managed to block out the fear that maybe he would never be good enough to make it. Now he was having it thrust into his face, presented as an undisputed fact.

"Face it, lad. Your mother's right."

"Look, you're good at lots of things," said his mother, trying to be positive. "You're doing well in class, your trumpet's coming along nicely and you write lovely stories. But – well, lets face it. When it comes to football…"

Henry was silent. His father tried another tack. "Look, when I was your age I longed to be a pilot. I used to dream of looping the loop. I even wrote off to the RAF. Then I went to Paris. I took one look from the top of the Eiffel Tower and fainted. Scared of heights, you see? So I had to accept that I was never going to make it as a pilot. It was a bitter pill to swallow but—"

"Striker!" It was Henry's favourite word. It conjured up images of winning, of glory, of coming out on top against all odds. It was all he could think of saying as his parents were closing in on him from both sides. "I am a striker!" he proclaimed.

"Get serious!" said his mother. "You're the worst shot in the world. Just look at the mat on the toilet floor! You've always fired miles wide of the mark."

His father went to put a consoling hand on his shoulder. But Henry was not at all ready to accept his parents' argument.

 "Henry Davis shrugs off one challenge and then a second. Undeterred by the verbal abuse of the crowd he lifts himself up and leaves."

With that Henry picked up his school bag and headed for the door.

 "But at the last minute he turns. Takes one look at his opponents and exclaims, in no uncertain terms: if you get a bike I'll sell it and buy my own boots!"

Henry made another dramatic exit.

CHAPTER 4

By the time Henry got to school, the morning kickabout had already started. He dropped his bag on top of the pile by the wall and ran to join in.

"To me!"

Gary had the ball. He played in goal for the school team because he loved diving about and getting muddy. He trapped the ball and passed it to Alan.

"Over here, Alan!"

Alan was the top scorer and the biggest boy in the school. People would take one look at him and ask, "Are you sure that lad is only eleven?" He flicked the ball up and headed it neatly to Ian.

"Ian, to me – on my head!"

Ian was the fastest runner in Holly Park School. His nickname was Speedo. He skilfully back-heeled the ball to Terry.

"Terry! Over here!"

Terry was the hard man of the team. His face was a permanent sneer. He put his foot on the ball and glared straight at Henry. "Here you are then!" he snarled and thumped the ball. Henry lunged a foot forward and missed. He crashed to the ground and the ball rolled away to the other end of the playground.

By the time Henry had picked himself up and collected the ball, the bell had gone for lining-up time.

"Bad luck," whispered Terry to Henry as they filed into school. "Maybe you'll actually touch the ball at playtime!"

School started, but to Henry and his friends classwork was merely a break between football matches. That did not mean they didn't work in class, because they did. It was just that school work was not that important. Well, nowhere near as important as football, anyway. This is something that all adults suspect and all children like Henry know – you come to school to play football. So Maths and English passed off without event, and before you could say "Diego Maradona" it was playtime.

Terry and Alan were always captains. No one knew exactly why, but it had been like that since the Infants.

"Gary..."

"Ian..."

"David..."

"Alison..."

It sounded just like registration, but in a different order. Henry wished that they really did use the class register to pick teams.

"Christopher..."

"Marcia..."

"Riccardo..."

"Lucy..."

At least alphabetical order had a kind of fairness to it. You don't often hear x, y or z complaining that they were last, and no one thinks that a, b and c are the best letters because they come first!

"Billy..."

"Philip..."

But the painful fact is that sides are picked in order of ability. It is so painful because it is so public. As each person is picked you can almost hear them thinking: Well, at least I'm better than—

"Julia..."

"Nicky..."

It was like torture. Henry knew he would be last. He always was. No matter how cool he tried to look or whether anyone made a comment or not he could still feel the weight of his friends' stares as they waited for the inevitable...

"I'd better have Henry then."

Playtime football is like no other game.

There is no referee, or clear pitch markings. Goals are of no fixed size with invisible crossbars and the rules are extremely flexible. There's never enough space and the size and type of ball depends entirely on whatever is available at the time. But it is played with the passion of a cup final.

"To me!"

Henry tried as hard as anyone to do well. Scoring a goal at playtime would be the highlight of his day.

"Over here – on my head!"

But it never happened.

"Tough luck," sniggered Terry as they lined up to go in. "Maybe you'll kick it at lunchtime play!"

He did. But then he had to collect it from the caretaker's house.

"Sorry, Mr Best. Can we have our ball back, please?"

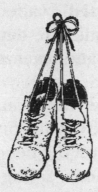

CHAPTER 5

Welcome to the dressing room at Holly Park School, where we have a rare behind-the-scenes glimpse of Henry Davis's pre-training preparations. He unzips his bag and lays out his kit with great care: first his shirt, then his shorts and finally his socks. He takes shallow breaths and clears his mind of all non-sporting thoughts. Slowly he warms up, going through the routine that has become his hallmark...

"Don't strain yourself!" called Terry from the other end of the hall. Tuesday after school was football practice and everyone was getting ready.

Henry ignored the comment. Nothing could deflect him from his preparations.

Terry sat down on the bench nearby. Henry was touching his toes, trying desperately not to bend his knees.

"I don't know why you bother!" Terry said.

Henry stretched his arms high above his head. He didn't flinch. Terry's little niggles were as much a part of his warm-up routine as the exercises.

"Right then, lads and lasses, gather round!" Mr Grace was in charge of the school team. To Henry he was the most important man alive. He alone had the power to choose who was good enough to play, who was in and who was out. Although he had so far failed to recognize Henry's talents it was never too late...

"Thank you all for coming. As you know

we have a big match next week – the cup semi-final against Winterton School. I am not going to pick the side today – that will be done after our Saturday morning training session. But I am going to be looking for extra effort. I want players who give one hundred and ten per cent. No matter who you are, you could get into the team if you show me that you really want to!"

Henry could feel the excitement simmering inside. No one wanted to get picked more than he did. It didn't matter that Mr Grace had made that same speech every Tuesday, Henry still hoped that today would be the day that everything went right, the day he would finally show just how good he was.

Mr Grace led the squad out on to the school field. Henry held back. He was always the last one out. This was not due to any superstition but because he always put his footwear on in private. He was ashamed of his threadbare plimsolls. As he pondered the big toe that poked out from the end, he was reminded of that morning's argument and the boots he longed for.

Luckily, the playing field was dry. The week before it had been so wet that Henry literally slipped over every time he lifted a foot.

CHAPTER 6

"Right! Terry and Alan pick teams," commanded Mr Grace.

"Gary ... Ian ... David ... Alison..."

"OK, here's the ball. I want to see thoughtful football. Lots of passing, running into space and people making themselves available. I don't want to see you all chasing the ball like a flock of geese at feeding time! This is a team game! Now off you go!"

Mr Grace rolled the ball towards the centre

and the game commenced.

"To me!... Over here!... On the wing!... Square ball!..."

Henry was desperate to catch Mr Grace's eye. If only he could do one thing to be noticed. Then he would be picked for the school team and at last a great footballing legend would be born. If only Mr Grace knew how easily *he* could become a national hero himself. He would be forever famous as the man who discovered Henry Davis!

"Great pass Alan!" called Mr Grace.

Henry was playing thoughtful football. He was running into space and making himself available. Unfortunately he was in a space that the ball was determined to avoid, and the rest of his team didn't care if he was available or not.

Mr Grace was waving his arms on the touch line. "Go on, Ian, cross it, lad! That's it!... Great header, Alan!... Oh, nice save, Gary! Great play!"

Henry watched the ball as it travelled around the pitch from player to player. He had given up calling for it and prepared himself for the inevitable moment of truth. It happened every Tuesday – the moment when, probably due to a misplaced pass, the ball would come straight at him. His chance to shine! All eyes would be on him! As he waited he whispered under his breath, "Just stay on your feet!"

And then it happened.

Henry was ready. He stood firm and braced himself as the ball looped high up in the air. It stayed there for ages. He quickly readjusted his position so that Mr Grace had a clear view of things. Henry decided to trap the ball, take it forward a few strides and send a chipped pass down the right wing for Ian to run on to. Behind him was Barry, his team's goalkeeper, calling for Henry to leave it. But he didn't have Henry's tactical brain. He couldn't see the space Ian was in. This would be a breath-taking manoeuvre that would surely mark the beginning of his rise to footballing stardom!

He took a step forward, trying to judge exactly where the ball was going to land.

"Leave it, Henry! It's mine!" screamed Barry, clearly alarmed at what his team mate was about to do. "Just get out of the way!"

 Davis quickly assesses the situation and realizes that there is a chance for a quick break down the right...

The ball was right in front of him now. He was in the perfect position. Well, almost perfect.

Henry held his foot just above the ground, hoping to bring the ball quickly under control. But he had misjudged where it was going to land and it slipped under his foot. Desperate to make up for this error he swung round to retrieve the ball and lunged at it. He made a solid connection with the ball and managed to thump it firmly. Unfortunately, he was now facing the wrong way and he sent the ball whizzing past the on-running goalkeeper. Henry had scored a spectacular own goal!

CHAPTER 7

"Not your day, was it, son?" Mr Best was sweeping up the clods of earth that always littered the floor after football practice. "Never mind, we all have days like that!"

Henry stuffed his kit into his bag. Everyone else had changed and left. He felt awful. An own goal! It was so embarrassing.

"I was watching," said the caretaker. "That Mr Grace – nice bloke, but he's got no idea about football. I wouldn't want him to train my pet dog let alone a school football team."

Henry zipped up his bag. He was not in the mood to discuss football, especially with someone who had just seen him score that own goal.

"When I was a lad we did nothing but play football. There was no TV in those days. We'd be out in the streets kicking a tin can about till we were called in. 'Course the streets were safer then."

Henry smiled politely and swung his bag over his shoulder. Mr Best didn't seem to require replies – he was leaning on his broom, staring into space. "I remember the first game my dad ever took me to: F.A. Cup Final, Wembley 1946. Derby County thrashed Charlton Athletic four–one. He won those tickets playing cards, otherwise we could never have afforded to go."

Henry started to move towards the door.

"I couldn't see a thing," Mr Best continued, "so I was passed overhead right down to the front. Imagine that happening nowadays!"

"Goodnight, Mr Best," said Henry.

"Haven't got any boots, have you, lad?"

Henry stopped dead in his tracks. He thought the caretaker had forgotten he was there. "No, I haven't."

"Pity that," said Mr Best. "You can't play football without football boots. It's like playing tennis without a racket!"

"Well, I might be getting a pair for my birthday," said Henry.

"When's that then?"

"In two weeks."

"That's not soon enough, is it? You need them by Saturday." Henry didn't know what to say.

"Come with me, young man..." Mr Best left the hall and Henry followed, puzzled. What was he doing? What did he want?

They got to the front door of the caretaker's house. "You wait here a minute," said Mr Best and he went inside. He re-emerged carrying a small battered case. It looked like an old fashioned doctor's bag. "Here, have these until you get your own pair."

Henry looked inside the bag. There, wrapped in newspaper, was a pair of football boots – not like the black shiny ones he wanted for this birthday, but a faded old brown pair. They looked more suited to climbing Mount Everest than to playing football.

"I know what you're thinking," said Mr Best, "and you're wrong. They may be old but these are quality boots. Take them home and try them."

Henry had never had a pair of football boots before. He really didn't know what to say.

"Go on, lad, take them. They've sat in my wardrobe for too long. It'll do them good to kick a ball again after all these years."

"Thank you," said Henry.

Henry Davis strolls home with his head held high. He knows that football is a tough sport. He's used to being the only one with any real faith in his own abilities and he knows that you have to take the bad times with the good. If you let a little thing like an own-goal get you downhearted, it's time to hang up your boots. And Henry Davis has no intention of doing that. In fact, he can't wait to get them on!

CHAPTER 8

"Hello Henry! You're a bit late. Anything wrong?"

His mother was the last person he wanted to talk to about the afternoon's events. She would only see it as more proof that he was never going to be a footballer. He decided to sit down at the table and eat his tea in silence.

"How did football training go, dear? Score any goals?"

Henry nearly choked on his crumpet.

"Are you all right, Henry? Here – have a glass of water."

Henry took a large gulp and resumed his silent munching. But he was on his guard now. He wasn't going to be tricked into talking, no matter how clever her questions were.

Henry's mother poured herself some tea and went to sit next to her son. "So, what did you learn in school today?"

Thousands of other school children up and down the country were probably being asked the same question right now, thought Henry. There should be a law against it! Don't parents know how unanswerable it is? Oh, how they would love to hear a stream of newly acquired facts flow from their children. A string of historical dates, a list of tricky spellings, the seven times table backwards or maybe that the capital of Italy is Rome, or that Henry VIII had six wives! He would have preferred to talk about the fussy seagulls that scavenged around for crisp crumbs at the end of breaktime and wouldn't touch the salt and vinegar ones. But he didn't. He took another biscuit and waited for the next most popular "interested parent" question…

"What did you have for lunch today?" There it was!

"Turkey and Christmas pudding!" snapped Henry. "I know it's March but Cook got the dates mixed up!"

"Very funny, Henry Davis!" said his mother. She got up and went to fetch a carrier bag. "I suppose you think that you can sulk your way to a pair of football boots. Well, you can forget that idea for a start." She tipped the contents of the bag on to the table. "Now flick through these and choose your birthday present."

Henry stared at the heap of bike magazines in front of him. Then he tidied them into one neat pile and carefully put them back in the carrier bag. "How many times have I told you not to leave your mess around the house?" he asked his mother.

"Fine!" she said. "If that's what you really want." She picked up the bag and dropped it into the bin. "There goes your birthday present!"

Henry Davis stands up from the table. Taking his half-eaten crumpet with him he makes his way to the door. He pauses to ponder whether he should turn and dramatically kick the bin over, but decides against it. Under extreme pressure he manages to keep his cool and leave the room with his dignity intact.

CHAPTER 9

Henry had hidden Mr Best's boots under his coat in the hall. It seemed the easiest thing to do. It was certainly easier than having to explain their existence to his mother. He grabbed the bag and ran upstairs to get ready. There was still about an hour of good daylight left.

He put his kit back on, saving the boots till last. Then he opened the black bag and removed the newspaper that surrounded them. It was old and faded. There were adverts for bars of soap and nylon stockings and a picture of a mangled old car being towed away by a truck. Henry folded the paper and slotted it back into the bag. Then he removed the boots. They were really quite heavy and the leather was very stiff. How can you play football in these? he thought.

But they were a surprisingly good fit. Henry walked about his bedroom as if he were in a shoe shop. They were comfortable and nowhere near as awkward as he expected.

He went downstairs very gingerly. The last thing he wanted to do was slip on the studs and collapse in a heap in the hall. Apart from the risk of injury he would have to explain his new footwear to his mother!

Henry Davis steps out on to the training ground. He knows it like his own back yard. In front of him are three upturned buckets the row of targets that he uses to sharpen his shooting skills. He delicately places the ball on the ground and takes two steps back.

Totally focused on where he intends to shoot, he strides forward and...

"Oh my God!"

Henry stood frozen, his mouth open. He could hardly believe it! He usually missed by miles, but there was the first bucket stuck in a rose bush. He had never kicked a ball like that before. Henry rushed to retrieve it, eager to try again. He stepped back and then swung his foot once more. The ball shot off like a cannonball and sent the second bucket flying.

"This is amazing!" he said to himself.

As he went to get the ball Henry felt a surge of power flow through his body. Two out of two – unheard of!

A hush descends. The faint-hearted turn away. Davis places the ball on the spot and prepares to achieve the impossible. He takes one step ... two ... and then...

"Yes!"

The third bucket almost cracked with the

force of the shot and Henry punched the air as if he had scored a last-minute penalty to win the cup. "I did it! I did it!" he yelled as he took a lap of honour around the lawn, acknowledging the cheers of his adoring fans (the daffodils).

Eventually he stopped and thought about what had just happened. Not only had he hit three targets in a row, he'd also belted the ball with so much power that he could still feel his foot throbbing inside the boot. Can a mere pair of football boots really make such a difference?

Henry collected the buckets and lined them up once more. This time he shot from further down the garden. But, like a pistol-twirling, sharpshooting cowboy, he shot them down again with frightening accuracy.

Henry decided to see what difference the boots would make to his close control. His record for keeping the ball off the ground was six and he had only managed that once.

He flicked the ball up. One ... two ... three...

...This is truly quite remarkable! It's as if the ball is attached to his foot by a thread...!

...four ... five ... six...

 ...This is an example of close control at its very best! The ball is like an obedient pet, responding perfectly to its master's commands. And Henry Davis is most definitely a master!

...seven ... eight ... nine...

Henry couldn't believe it. In front of him the ball was performing tricks he had never seen before. It bobbed gently from foot, to knee, to foot, to head, to shoulder and back to foot again as if it had decided to do it itself!

...sixteen ... seventeen ... eighteen...

How could this have happened?

...nineteen ... twenty...

Henry balanced the ball in the curve of his foot, flicked it up and powered a stunning volley across the garden. It cracked like thunder against the goal that was painted on the back of the garage.

Something very peculiar was going on. Somewhere deep inside, a chrysalis was forming...

CHAPTER 10

"Are you coming down for supper or am I going to have to throw your food away?"

Henry sat on the edge of his bed staring at the boots.

"Henry Davis, I have had enough of your moods. Come down here at once or you can forget your birthday completely!"

Henry gave the boots one last hug and placed them carefully back in their bag. "Thank you," he whispered to them as he slid the bag under his bed.

"...And about time too! This food is practically cold! And why haven't you taken those filthy clothes off? You're getting mud all over the floor. What were you doing up there? Daydreaming, no doubt. Well, I tell you, Henry Davis, you had better liven your ideas up, my lad. I've just about had enough of your cheekiness!"

"Yes, Mum. Sorry, Mum,"

"And another thing. Your room is a tip. I'm fed up with picking up your underwear. Don't you know where the dirty linen basket is?"

"Sorry, Mum. I'll tidy it up straight after supper—"

"And while I mention it..." Then she stopped. "What did you say?"

"I'll tidy up my room, I promise. Straight after supper, just before my bath."

Henry's mother sat down at the table. "Why?"

Henry carefully pushed some peas on to the back of his fork and guided them into his mouth. "What do you mean?" he replied.

"Why are you going to tidy your room?"

"Because you asked me," Henry replied.

His mother stared deep into his face. "What are you after, Henry Davis? What do you want? Is this a new ploy to get a pair of football boots? Do you think that being an angel for a few days will change our minds?"

"No, Mum. Honest!" said Henry. "Anyway I don't want a pair of boots any more."

Henry's mother was stunned. "What did you say? Are my ears playing tricks? Is this some kind of a joke?"

"No, I promise. I don't want you to buy me a pair of football boots. I mean it."

"Well, knock me down with a feather!" she said. "Talk about changing your tune!"

Henry ate his final pea and placed his knife and fork neatly on his plate. "Please may I leave the table?"

"Yes. Off you go…" Henry's mother was still very confused. Was this the same boy who had stormed out this morning?

CHAPTER 11

Upstairs Henry was as good as his word. By the time his father got home his room was tidy, he was clean and he had finished his homework.

"Well now," said his father as he sat next to Henry on the settee, "how was your day?"

Henry looked up into his father's face. "It was really great! We learnt that the Vikings first landed in England in AD793 and that William the Conqueror was the last one to invade us in 1066. I can now do my seven times table forwards and backwards, and I learnt how to spell Egypt, pneumonia and chrysanthemum!"

"That's really quite impressive!" said his father. "And your mother ... er ... told me that ... well, you've had a change of heart over your birthday present."

"That's right," said Henry. "I no longer want you to buy me a pair of football boots."

"And ... er ... why exactly is that? I mean, after you had set your heart on a pair ... and after this morning and everything..."

Henry paused and then sniffed dramatically. "It's what happened at football practice," he replied. "I scored an own goal. It was terrible!"

Henry buried his head in his father's stomach. This was because, although he was brilliant at sounding as if he was crying, he never could produce good fake tears. He always screwed his face up too much. Such a giveaway!

His mother sat down beside him. "You

didn't tell me, Henry. And there I was, shouting at you like that!"

Henry didn't dare move his head. Things were going far too well.

"Sometimes it takes a dreadful event like this to help us see sense," said his mother. "At least now you know that football just isn't for you."

Henry didn't move.

"That's right," continued his dad. "Every cloud has a silver lining."

Henry still didn't move.

"Just think. No more jokes about you falling over. No more disappointment when you don't get picked for the school team..."

Henry got ready to move.

"And think of all the money you'll save on those silly football magazines!" said his mum.

Henry moved! He shot up and charged out of the room, bawling like a baby. He stormed upstairs and slammed his door. Then he quietly pushed it open again to make sure that his wails of anguish carried all the way downstairs.

It took ten minutes of sobbing, bellowing and blubbering before his mother came up to comfort him. "Don't take it so hard," she said. "Look, I've saved all those bike magazines from the bin. Let's look through them together."

Henry's head was buried in his pillow. "I didn't say I was giving up football," he muffled. "I only said I didn't want a pair of boots."

"'But Henry, what about the own goal?"

"It's just not fair!" Henry blubbered. "You never listen to me!"

Three deep sobs, a long sniff, one final blubber, then some gentle whimpering. Now he was ready for the big finish. But it had to be timed to perfection...

"You just don't care about me!"

"Of course I do!" said his mother, clearly distressed.

 Yes! Henry Davis pulls off this complicated manoeuvre with remarkable skill. His mother is now on the defensive and

Henry is about to finish the move...

"Then let me go to Saturday morning's training session. Mr Grace will be picking the team for next week's semi-final against Winterton."

"Well, I ... er..." His mother was totally defenceless.

In a flash Henry was hugging his mother. "Oh please, Mum! I'm sorry I said you didn't care. I really am! And I promise that if I don't get into the team on Saturday I'll never kick a ball again!"

 What a move! But has the ball crossed the line? Everyone waits for the decision of the referee...

"Oh, all right." Henry's mother gave him a hug and a kiss, and then left.

YES! WHAT A FANTASTIC GOAL!

Henry reached under his bed, hugged and

kissed the black leather bag and whispered to the boots, "This is it!"

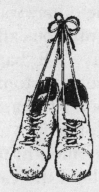

CHAPTER 12

The question was, would Henry's dad notice the boots? As he sat in the back of the car on the way to school, Henry was pretty sure he wouldn't.

"Thanks for bringing me. I know how you like a lie-in on Saturdays," said Henry.

"Your mother insisted," said his father. "She wanted me to be there to hear that you haven't been picked."

"Well thanks for the vote of confidence!"

As the car pulled into the school car park Henry could see the others warming up. What Terry had said the previous afternoon was still fresh in his memory: "Oi, banana feet! Don't waste your time coming tomorrow! Go and play for Winterton! At least you'd have a chance of scoring for us!"

You just wait, big mouth! thought Henry.

Henry's father held the car door open for him.

"See you, Dad!"

"Good luck!" called his father.

As he ran towards the school he wondered if his dad really meant it.

"So you made it," said Gary.

"It's about all he's going to make," said Terry. "My gran's got more chance of getting into this team than him and she's eighty-four and half-blind!"

Henry smiled to himself.

No one noticed Henry's boots because no one ever really noticed Henry. The truth was, he could have been wearing a pair of diver's flippers and nobody would have commented.

"Good morning!" called Mr Grace. "Nice of you all to come. Before we start let me say that I would dearly love to pick all of you for the team but it's just not possible." Henry could hear Terry's suppressed giggle. "So I don't want the unlucky ones to be too disappointed."

It's funny how teachers' voices change, thought Henry. Not that Mr Grace is normally a stern man but he was definitely more polite when he was in front of parents.

"Before we have a game, we'll have a spot of shooting practice to warm you all up."

 Henry Davis moves off, his jet black hair bobbing up and down as he jogs. His slight frame belies his total determination...

"Right, let's get started. Gary, you get in goal... OK, everyone else line up. I'll roll a ball, you shoot first time then run back to the end of the line and so on...

The squad lines up. Davis finds himself at the

*back. He hops from foot to foot as he moves
towards the front...*

"Nice shot, Alan... Good try, Alison. Next time keep your head down... Well done, Ian, but don't snatch at it..."

Henry Davis prepares himself. It's crucial to decide beforehand just where you want to put it – top right-hand corner, he decides...

"Nice try, Terry... Great save, Gary... OK, Henry, it's your turn..."

No one was really paying attention because no one ever did when Henry was playing. Mr Grace rolled the ball in front of him and Henry swung his foot at it with all his might.

For a moment the world stood still. At first it was the thwack of boot on ball that stunned everyone. Then there was a shared disbelief as all those present looked at each other to confirm that they had all seen the same thing.

"Cracking shot, Henry!" said Mr Grace.

Davis returns to the end of the line. Top right-hand corner he had said, and top right-hand corner it was!

Henry tried to catch his father's eye but he was nowhere to be seen. He turned to look at the car park and there he was, in the car reading his newspaper. Well, at least he hasn't seen the boots, thought Henry.

 The atmosphere becomes charged as Davis's second shot approaches. Once more he picks his spot early – bottom left-hand corner...

"OK, Henry, here we go..." The ball was rolled.

A loud "Wow!" greeted the shot as it nestled into the corner of the net. "Great shot!" called somebody else's father.

"Er, nice one, Henry!" said Mr Grace. Like everyone else who had ever seen Henry Davis try to kick a ball, he was totally flummoxed.

As he trotted back to his place, Henry

felt a pat on his back. "Great shooting!" said Alan.

"Thanks," said Henry coolly. But inside he was exploding.

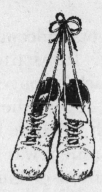

Chapter 13

"OK, we'll have the same sides as Tuesday's football practice," called Mr Grace. "Now remember – run into space, make yourself available and play as a team."

Henry noticed his father strolling up from the car park. You're in for a shock, he thought. But he wasn't the only one who was about to be surprised.

Henry's feet began to tingle. At first he thought it was just because he wasn't used to wearing boots, but it wasn't really that kind of tingle.

As the game got underway Henry's toes began to twitch. His feet started to throb and the tingle got much stronger and rose up through his body. It was the same surge of power that he'd felt when he had first put on the boots, but this time it was much stronger.

Meanwhile, in front of him Henry's team mates were ignoring him as they always did.

"Over here ... to me..."

Maybe they thought those thunderbolt shots were just lucky strikes...

"Here! Over here!"

...but things were about to change!

 The ball is cleared from defence and lands at the feet of Terry Devlin, the big burly centre half. Henry Davis is well-placed to his left and calls for the ball... Devlin turns to play the ball back to his goalkeeper... Davis has other ideas! He sprints with lightning speed towards his captain and takes the ball, looks up, sees a gap and charges into it. He

swerves past one defender, leaps over the lunge of another ... the ball sticks like a magnet to his feet as he quickly turns to avoid one last desperate challenge. He's on the edge of the box... He looks up and sends a deft chip over the outcoming goalkeeper... The ball glides elegantly into the back of the net. What a goal!

Henry punched the air in delight. For a moment no one reacted. The world had stopped once more. But then he was swamped by a pile of ecstatic team mates!

"Great goal!... Brilliant!... Fantastic!"

One by one Mr Grace dismantled the mountain of children. "Come on, back to the centre..." He carried on digging until he got to Henry. He leant down and helped the goal scorer to his feet. "That was amazing!" he said. "How did you do it?"

Henry just shrugged and jogged back to his position. On the touchline the fathers were still applauding. All except one. Henry's father was catching flies with his mouth!

The game got underway again...

Davis is seeing a lot of the ball. The game is revolving around him now. He collects it in the centre circle, evades a tackle and flicks the ball wide to Ian Mantovani who charges down the wing. With breath-taking pace Davis sprints forward... Mantovani floats a high cross into the box... Davis rises between two defenders, meets the ball firmly with his head and fires it like a bullet into the net! A brilliant goal!

This time the reaction was instant. Once more Henry was engulfed and Mr Grace had to go looking for him.

Henry's father had stopped catching flies. He had stopped doing anything. He looked as if he'd been turned to stone!

"What did you have for breakfast this morning?" asked Mr Grace as they trotted back to the centre.

Henry smiled to himself. He had never felt so good.

...into the last minute now, and there's a free kick just outside the box. Devlin stands over the ball...

"Let me take it, Terry!" Henry whispered.

"Shove off, Banana Feet!" snapped Terry.

 ...he places it down as the defensive wall gets into position...

"I'll score, Terry. I know it!"

"Go away or this ball won't be the only thing I kick!"

 ...Devlin lines up his shot, takes his run up and belts the ball straight into the wall. It lofts high in the air and comes to Davis. He chests it down, flicks it up with his knee and cracks a looping volley high into the net! A hat trick!

This time Mr Grace joined in the congratulations along with a group of excited fathers. Suddenly Henry was lifted up from the crush

and placed on his team mates' shoulders.
Henry really was on top of the world.

CHAPTER 14

Mr Best was leaning on the car park gate, waiting to lock up.

In the back of the car Henry's heart sank. It had been a perfect morning. His dad hadn't noticed the boots. But there was Mr Best, about to ruin everything!

Henry's father pulled up alongside the caretaker and wound his window down.

"How's tricks then, Mr Davis?"

"Fine, and how are you?"

"All the better for watching your lad this morning. He played a blinder!"

"He certainly did!" replied the proud dad.

"What's your secret, lad?" asked Mr Best, poking his head through the window.

Henry couldn't speak. He just waited for the inevitable bombshell.

"How are the boots then?" There it was!

"What boots?" asked Henry's father.

"The boots I gave him on Tuesday. Couldn't have him playing on an important day like this without boots, now, could we?"

The car was suddenly filled with a highly charged silence.

"What with his birthday being after the semi-final," added Mr Best. "That would have been too late!"

Henry's father slowly turned round and pulled open the bag on his son's lap to reveal the boots. "You're quite right, Mr Best. It would have been far too late," he said.

"Well, can't hang around chatting," said the caretaker. "I've got a steak and kidney pie waiting for me. " 'Bye now!" Henry's father drove off in silence. But not for long...

"'I don't want you to buy me boots, Mummy dear... I'm sorry I was so rude, Mummy dear... I'll tidy my room, I'll wash the car, I'll do the dishes, Mummy dear!'"

Henry sank down in his seat.

"I'll go begging for boots, Mummy dear... I'll say what cruel and stingy people my parents are, Mummy dear!"

"No, it wasn't like that!" pleaded Henry. "I didn't go begging for them. He just gave them to me."

The car came to a sudden halt and Henry's father turned around. His massive face filled the gap between the two front seats.

"You're telling me that, completely out of the blue, someone walks up to you and gives you a pair of football boots! What kind of fool do you take me for?"

Jeffrey Davis didn't get angry often. But when he did...

"God knows how many people you went grovelling to before you found Mr Best!"

"No! You've got it wrong!" There were real

tears in Henry's eyes now. "He was watching the practice on Tuesday and then gave them to me. I didn't ask for them! I promise!"

"Don't give me any of your promises!" snapped Henry's father. "They're not worth the breath you use to make them!"

Henry burst into tears.

"Wait until your mother hears about this!"

Henry felt his world crumbling about him. He had played like a star, won the respect of all his team-mates and been picked to play in the school team. Now it was all going to be taken away from him.

By the time they got back home Henry had stopped crying but his eyes were as red as radishes. "Out you come!" growled his father. Henry slunk out of the car, dragging his bag behind him.

His mother must have been waiting by the window. She came bursting out of the front door and lunged at Henry with a huge hug. "Never mind, dear. It's all over now. Don't you worry yourself about silly old football! Who cares about a stupid school team?"

"I think you'd better sit down," said Henry's father. "Things aren't quite what they seem."

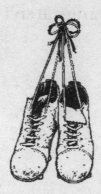

CHAPTER 15

Mr Davis handed his wife a cup of tea. Henry stood sheepishly by the back door.

"What's wrong?" asked his mother. "What's going on?"

"Your son," started Mr Davis. "Your son has stunned me!"

"Why? What has he done?"

"I never thought I'd live to see a day like this one!"

"Tell me what you're talking about," said

Mrs Davis.

"This boy frankly shocked me today!" Mr Davis went to put a hand on Henry's shoulder. "He played football like I've never seen before! He scored a hat trick! He was brilliant! He was a star!"

Then, to both Henry and his mother's surprise, Mr Davis started to skip around the kitchen. He leapt over a chair, picked up a broom and twirled it around as if it were a dancing partner.

"Have you gone mad?" shouted Henry's mother.

"No!" came the reply. "I'm just amazed!" He spun the broom around one more time, dropped it to the floor and stepped up on to the kitchen table. "Our son!" he shouted. "Our son has been picked for the school team to play Winterton in the semi-final of the Schools' Cup!"

"I don't believe it!" said Henry's mother, finally getting the message.

"Well, you better had!" said her husband, and he jumped off the table, landed just in front of his wife and planted a massive kiss on her cheek. Then he was off around the kitchen again. "We're gonna win the cup! We're gonna win the cup! For now you've gotta belie-ieve us … we're gonna win the cup!"

"Hold on!" screamed Henry's mother. "Let me get this straight. Our son, Henry Davis, the boy who couldn't kick his way out of a paper bag, has been picked for the school team?"

"Got it in one!" said Henry's father.

Mrs Davis sat back down again. This was clearly a big shock to her. An even bigger shock than seeing her huge husband leaping around the kitchen like an electrocuted rabbit!

"Then why was he crying?" she asked. "I'd have thought he'd be pleased as punch!"

Henry didn't know what was going to happen now. After watching his father's display of kitchen gymnastics, anything was possible!

"He was," said Mr Davis, doing his best to calm down. "He was over the moon. But then he thought of you."

"And that made him burst into tears?"

"Yes... I mean, no... Well, sort of. You see, he thought you would be so upset that he'd got into the team that you would ban him from playing anyway. I said that you would never be that cruel, but he wouldn't believe me. So go on, tell him! Tell him how proud you are of him! Tell him that he can play in the school team! Go on, tell him!"

Henry held his breath.

"Of course I'm pleased, Henry," stuttered his mother. "I know how important it is to you. And if it's important to you, it's important to me." She gave her son another huge hug.

This family has become very physical lately, thought Henry.

CHAPTER 16

"Why did you do it, Dad?"

Henry and his father had gone upstairs "to discuss tactics".

"Because," said Mr Davis, "she would have gone mad."

"But you went mad in the car!"

"Yes. But *I* didn't stop you from playing in the school team!"

Suddenly Henry understood. "Thanks, Dad," and he ran to give his father a hug.

"I had no idea that you had improved so much, Henry. You were absolutely brilliant!" He turned to go downstairs.

"What shall we say about the boots?" asked Henry.

"Boots?" said his father. "What boots? You're in the team now. That's all that matters."

As his father left the room Henry lay back on his bed with relief. His kit bag was on the floor and he leaned across to take out the boots. The mud from this morning was quite dry now and easy to break off. As he picked away Henry started to think. What if it really was only the boots? Why did his feet tingle and his toes twitch? Were these really magic boots?

Of course not! That's ridiculous ... isn't it?

Henry began to worry. He had to admit that this rapid improvement in form was hard to explain. He always knew he had it in him, but how could a simple pair of boots bring it out?

And if it *was* just the boots, what would

happen when he played in the playground with his old trainers?

He thought about going into the garden right then to try and hit the targets without the boots. That would settle it once and for all. But he couldn't. While he knew that the very idea of boots with magical powers was crazy, a little voice at the back of his head kept saying they might be.

Once he had scrubbed them clean, Henry held the boots in his hand. They didn't look magical – not that he knew what magical boots would look like. If anything they were plain. He inspected them closely: nothing but leather and stitching. He began to giggle to himself. Magic boots indeed! If he rubbed them hard enough, would a genie come out? "I am the genie of the boot! I grant you three wishes, oh master!"

Henry laughed and put the boots back in their black bag. He covered them with the old piece of newspaper and pushed the bag under his bed. "You rest there, my friends," he said. "I'll see you on semi-final day!"

CHAPTER 17

"What's wrong with your leg, Henry?"

"Oh no! Our star player is injured!"

"What happened?"

"It's just a strain," Henry replied. "Honestly, it's nothing!"

And "honestly" it really was nothing. On the way to school Henry had decided to develop a limp. It was the only way he could think of avoiding the possible humiliation of playground football.

"The doctor said if I rest it for a day it will be fine. I'll be OK for tomorrow's game."

The news of Henry's fabulous trial had spread through the playground. Infant children who didn't even know him wanted to watch him play. "Do some tricks! Do some tricks!" they called.

"Look, I'm really sorry," he said to the gathering crowd. "I just can't risk it. Tomorrow's a very important game."

"He's right," said Alan. "If there's even the slightest chance that he doesn't play tomorrow it would be a disaster!"

"Henry just has to be fit!" said Ian.

"Don't worry, lads, I will be," said the wounded hero as he limped off to the cloakroom.

Henry hung his coat on his peg.

"What's up, lad? Boots too tight, were they?" It was Mr Best.

"No. I just strained my leg in the garden yesterday. It's nothing too serious."

Henry was suddenly consumed with curiosity. He had to ask something.

"Were they your old boots?"

"Not exactly," answered Mr Best. "They were given to me."

"Oh!" Henry responded, trying to sound as disinterested as he could. "How old are they?"

"Let's see now. I got them nearly forty years ago now!"

Henry was shocked. "Forty years! That's older than my dad!"

"Comfortable, are they?"

"Er … yes. Thank you. But don't you want them back?"

"Oh, you keep them as long as you need to," replied the caretaker. "I know they're in good hands. Or should I say good feet?" Mr Best chuckled off down the corridor.

"What's this I hear?" Mr Grace came into the cloakroom. "What have you done?"

"Nothing … honestly … it's just a strain. I'll be fine tomorrow."

"Has a doctor seen it?"

"Er … yes. He said I should rest it."

Mr Grace looked anxiously at Henry's leg.

"Well, you'd better take it easy today."

Henry made his way to his classroom. Limping was somehow easier now he was carrying the weight of all those lies.

CHAPTER 18

Henry leaned out of bed and removed the boots from their bag. Then he slid back and pulled the duvet over his head.

"Today's the day!" he whispered to the boots in the darkness of his bed. "Our first proper match! A semi-final in front of the whole school!" He clutched them tightly to his chest. "I don't know if you're magic, but today I don't really care. All I know is that we're going to win!"

There was a knock at the door.

"Are you getting up?" called his mother. "You're going to be late."

Oh no I'm not! Henry thought, and he leapt out of bed fully dressed in his school uniform. He looked in the mirror – no one would know that he'd slept in it! He quickly packed the boots into his kit bag and dashed into the bathroom just as his mother was coming out.

"You got dressed quickly!"

"I'm in a hurry, Mum. Today's the day!"

Henry's mother had resigned herself to the fact that football was still the most important thing in her son's life.

Henry wolfed down an extra bowl of cereal. He kissed his mum, said goodbye and charged towards the front door. An envelope was wedged inside the letter box with his name on. He opened it. *Good luck in the semi-final! Love from Dad*. He tucked the note into his pocket and left.

"How's the leg?" asked Alan as he arrived at school.

"Sorry? Oh, yes ... er ... fine, thanks."

Time passed so slowly. Henry was sure the class clock needed a new battery: every time he looked at it the hands had hardly moved!

The kick-off was at two o'clock on the school field. Mrs Thorne, the head teacher, had allowed the whole junior school to watch. "It is not every day that we are one step away from a final!" she had said in assembly. The whole school even said a prayer "for a good sporting game, and may the best team win. Amen".

"That's us!" Ian had whispered through his hands.

At lunchtime Mr Grace called the squad together.

"Right then, let's start preparing now. Remember the golden rules: concentrate, play as a team, stick to your positions and move into space!" Everyone looked as if they were hanging onto his every word, but they weren't. While he was going on about space, awareness and commitment every child was thinking of one thing and one thing only – "We're one step away from the final!"

"...and don't start shooting from too far out. Remember, we play a passing game and if we get that right the chances will flow..."

Holly Park had never got this far in the Schools' Cup before!

"...and remember to use the width of the pitch. Get the ball right to the touch-lines – it'll stretch their defence and create gaps that our midfield players can exploit..."

And the final is going to be at Highfield Rovers! A real football ground with proper nets and professional changing rooms! There'll be loads of people there and the local newspaper...

"...so stay calm. Just concentrate on the game. Don't go thinking about the final until you've done the job today!"

...Just think: the Schools' Cup Final at Highfield Rovers! Brill!

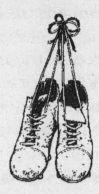

CHAPTER 19

"Holly, Holly, Holly Park!
Holly Park, Holly Park!
Holly, Holly, Holly Park!
Holly, Holly Park!"

...and welcome to Holly Park School, the home of football! The crowd is buzzing with excitement at the prospect of a thrilling School's Cup semi-final between the home side and Winterton School. Conditions here

are perfect for good football – a credit to Mr
Best, the groundsman, and all his staff!

The pitch was framed by the red and green of
the Holly Park school uniform. Winterton had
brought along a few supporters but they were
far too outnumbered to be heard.

*A mighty roar greets the teams as
they come out on to the pitch. The two
sides met earlier this season in the
League, where Winterton ended up one–nil
winners. So in normal circumstances they
should be favourites, but these are not normal
circumstances! Since that game Holly Park have
introduced a new player into their side – Henry
Davis, the name on everybody's lips! Will he
produce the same form that won him a place on
the side?*

Terry trotted up to shake hands with the
opposing captain. As he went past Henry he
snarled. Terry was a good footballer, but a
terrible sportsman. He was the best footballer

at Holly Park – everyone knew that. Until now!

 Winterton kick off, defending the goal nearest the nursery block...

Henry's feet began to tingle. He was half expecting them to.

...it's a slow start, which is only to be expected in such an important game. Neither side wants to be the first to make a mistake. Winterton have the ball and loft it high into Holly Park territory. It's collected by Davis – he looks up – Winterton's marking is very tight – there's no one free. He moves forward – sees a gap – twenty-five metres out – surely he's not going to shoot! He does – GOAL!

A mighty roar greeted the goal and Henry was mobbed once more.

Henry's strike sent shock waves through the opposition. How were they going to stop someone who could hit the ball from so far out?

Winterton's once well-organized defence panics as they struggle to contain Davis. Two players charge towards him as he collects the ball in midfield. They lunge at him together – he gently flicks the ball up and over their challenge and leaves them floundering on the ground. Oceans of space open up in front of him – a third defender tries to close him down – Davis waits – plays a sweet pass into the gap that has opened up – Mantovani runs on to it and simply chips it over the outcoming keeper. Two–nil!

> *"Holly, Holly, Holly Park!*
> *Holly Park, Holly Park!*
> *Holly, Holly, Holly Park!*
> *Holly, Holly Park!"*

The half-time whistle blew. The crowd went wild apart from the Winterton supporters, who were in shock!

"You're playing like stars!" said Mr Grace. "And I reckon you've got magic in those boots,

Henry Davis!"

It was only a joke but it sent shivers down Henry's spine.

 The second half gets underway and Winterton have it all to do!

Magic boots or not, Henry dominated the game. The crowd had stopped worrying about the result and started chanting "Henry! Henry!"

Winterton are desperately trying to make a game of it. They've forced a corner and sent everyone but the goalkeeper into the Holly Park box. The ball swings into the centre – a Winterton head meets it and sends it towards the top left-hand corner – it must be a ... no! A foot shoots upwards – with a remarkable overhead kick Davis clears the ball from under the cross bar and sends it towards the half-way line. Devlin is clear – he has the entire Winterton half at his mercy. It has to be ... it is!

Wintertons' hearts sank. They knew there was nothing they could do. When the final whistle went they were relieved it was only five–nil!

Henry was a hero. The feeling that the rest of the world was beginning to recognize his talent filled him with excitement.

CHAPTER 20

"We're playing St John's," said Mr Grace.

The news was greeted with silence. St John's had been the cup holders for the last two years and were the biggest school in the competition. Earlier in the year they had thrashed Holly Park four–one, and that was with their B team!

"Still, with Henry in our team, we must have a chance!"

"And the day has been changed. The final

is next Tuesday – Highfield Rovers now have a game on the Saturday."

"Tuesday's my birthday!" said Henry.

"Then we'll have a party!" said Alan.

Back home Henry's mother greeted the news with disappointment. "But we so wanted to have a proper tea! Uncle Arthur and Aunt Linda did so want to come," she said. "Now the whole day will be dominated by football!"

But his father was really pleased about it. "Invite the whole family to the match! I can't think of a better place than Highfield Rovers to celebrate a birthday!"

Henry didn't really care. He would have gladly swapped his birthday for a winner's medal there and then!

"Did you know that Mr Best used to play for them?" asked Henry's father. "Almost forty years ago now."

"Mr Best played for Highfield?" Henry was astonished. "Did you ever see him play?"

"No. He hung up his boots long before I was born." The mention of boots turned Henry cold again! "If I remember rightly, his career was cut short by an injury."

Henry was fascinated. He couldn't wait to get to school to ask Mr Best more.

He was ready so early the next morning that he actually had breakfast with his father.

"And to what do I owe this honour?" said Mr Davis, passing Henry the milk.

"I've got a bit of homework to do," Henry replied. "Research on our Vikings project."

Henry waited until his father had left for work, then gathered up his school things. "I'm off now, Mum," he called. "I promised to help Mrs Thorne sort out the PE equipment."

As Henry walked to school he marvelled at how good he'd become at telling lies. The PE equipment! he thought. Now, where did that idea come from?

Mr Best was sweeping the playground. "Good morning, lad! You're a bit early today."

"Am I? Oh. Our clocks at home must be running fast." He dashed to the cloakroom and back again in record time. "Mr Best, my dad said you used to play for Highfield Rovers."

Mr Best stopped sweeping and leaned on his broom. He suddenly looked rather thoughtful. "That was a long time ago, lad."

"What position did you play?"

"Left back," Mr Best replied. "Left back in the changing rooms!"

Henry laughed. "What was it like?"

Mr Best looked straight at Henry, and sighed. "Oh, those days have long gone!" He carried on sweeping.

"Henry Davis!" a familiar voice called from the school building. It was Mrs Thorne. "Why are you at school so early? Have the clocks gone wrong in your house? Well, it's a good thing you're here; you can help me tidy up the PE equipment. It's been left in a terrible mess!"

So much for lying, thought Henry.

Chapter 21

"Have you got any books about Highfield Rovers?"

Henry liked coming to the local library. It was enormous. He often popped in on his way home from school. There were always lots of very serious people sitting at tables reading books. They all looked very clever and important. Henry loved taking a book and sitting at a table with it. Anyone seeing him would think what a clever, important boy he was!

"Here's one," said the librarian, *The History of Highfield Rovers*. It's a bit out of date now; would you like me to find you a more modern book?"

"No. That will be fine, thank you," Henry replied. He gave the man his ticket and put the book in his bag.

"Where have you been?" asked his mum when he got home. "Don't tell me – the PE equipment was messy again."

"I went to the library on the way home," Henry replied. "I had to get a book out for our Vikings homework." He rushed upstairs. "I'll go and do it now before tea!" he called down.

Henry flicked through the book. He found a chapter entitled Stars of the Fifties. He sat on his bed and read:

The fifties were successful years for Highfield Rovers. They reached two Wembley finals and challenged hard for the league. Under the inspired management of Bob Matthews, their powerful young squad made Rovers one of the toughest teams in the country...

"Your tea's ready, Henry. Come down now."

...Surely the superstar of the team was the great Davey Evans. He was heralded as the most gifted player in the land. He played for England when he was only nineteen years old and was tipped by many to be a future captain of his country...

"Hurry up! It's getting cold."

...but tragedy struck in 1958 when he was killed in a car crash. The country mourned the loss of a hero and many say that Highfield Rovers football club has never really recovered from it. Driving the car was Rovers defender, Rodney Best...

"If you don't come down right now, I'm going to give your food to next door's cat!"

Best suffered light injuries in the crash. He was a talented young left back and close friend of Evans. He never regained his confidence and retired from the game two years later.

"This is your last warning, Henry Davis!"

Henry put the book down and got the black boot bag out from under his bed. He took out the piece of old newspaper that the boots were wrapped in. Under the picture of the mangled car was written:

The wreck of Rodney Best's car being towed away from yesterday's tragic accident. Best was taken to hospital with minor leg injuries but his passenger, the talented midfield player, Davey Evans, died instantly. Police aren't currently able to say what caused the crash...

Henry suddenly felt very cold. He also felt very guilty. He had found out something that he wasn't meant to. Not that it was a secret – the whole country knew about it forty years ago. But no one had actually told him. If Mr Best had wanted him to know, then surely he would have said. Henry remembered the thoughtful look on the caretaker's face earlier that day and felt very sad.

He got out the boots. Mr Best had said that they were given to him. Henry knew, now, who they'd belonged to.

Later that night Henry showed his dad the book. They found a team photograph with Rodney Best sitting, arms folded, in the front row. "He must have had tiny feet if he gave those boots to you!" Mr Davis whispered to Henry, pointing at the picture.

Henry didn't say anything.

"What are you two looking at?" asked Mrs Davis.

"It's just a book Henry got out from the library," said Mr Davis, and he handed it to his wife.

"Oh yes. Tell me, Henry Davis, since when have Vikings played football for Highfield Rovers?"

CHAPTER 22

Henry was awake long before daylight shone through his window. It was Cup Final day. It was also his birthday, but his thoughts were all on the game. Beside him in his bed were the boots. It didn't seem to him to be at all strange to have hugged a pair of boots all night.

For two weeks now he had managed to avoid ever kicking a ball without these boots on. He had volunteered to stay in and help tidy up the classroom at playtime so often that he had earned a new nickname, "the Sweeper". He had joined every lunchtime club there was: recorder club, chess club and even the infant choir. ("I'll help them with the tricky bits, Miss!" he'd pleaded with the music teacher.) He had managed to resist the demands of his friends to join in a kickabout by insisting that he didn't want to aggravate his injury and that he wanted to save himself for "the big one".

Well, today was the "the big one"!

"Happy birthday!" called his parents as he entered the kitchen. The room was decorated with balloons and streamers and a pile of cards sat neatly next to his cereal bowl.

"Come on, lad, eat up! You're going to need all your energy this afternoon." His father had taken the day off work especially to be at the final.

Henry tried to peep out of the back window. He was sure that the red bike would be there. When he couldn't see it he decided that his dad had probably thought it was best to keep the surprise until after the game, rather than take his mind off things beforehand.

The phone hardly stopped ringing until the moment he left for school. Most of Henry's relations called to wish him a happy birthday and say that they were looking forward to seeing him play that afternoon. "There'll be so many members of our family there," said Henry's mother, "it'll be like Christmas!"

The playground was full of tension. There was nervous excitement everywhere. Even the infants were talking about "the big singer" (their nickname for Henry ever since he had joined their choir).

Mrs Thorne had declared the day "Our Cup Final day!"

"We can put our maths and our English to one side for the day," she had said in assembly. "Today is a historic day for Holly Park and, win or lose, the memory will live with us for ever!"

At lunchtime the playground looked like a shopping centre car park. Transport had been organized to take the entire school in convoy to Highfield Rovers. The sight of so many cars, bedecked in red and green, brought hoards of people out on to the street. By the time the convoy arrived at the ground it had doubled in size.

Similar scenes occurred five miles away round the streets of St John's School. So with half an hour to go until kick-off the ground was awash with red and green on one side, and blue and white on the other. Flags and scarves waved frantically and rows of painted faces chanted at the tops of their voices.

CHAPTER 23

If the atmosphere in the stadium was highly charged, the electricity being generated in the Holly Park changing room was enough to supply a small city for a week!

"Now, I want you all to enjoy the afternoon. This is a once-in-a-lifetime chance. Imagine! You are actually about to play in a top class stadium on a perfect pitch! It'll be something you could tell your grandchildren..." Mr Grace was almost choked up with emotion.

But his team were not on his wavelength. He was talking as a thirty-seven-year-old football enthusiast who had become a teacher. Any sporting ambitions he might have had when he was young had been discarded along with his round, metal-framed glasses and his grey turned-up shorts. To the children who sat obediently in front of him, any adult who didn't play top class professional football was ... well, a failed top class professional footballer. But *they* could never be described as that. It might be the first time that any of these children had played in such a stadium but it was unthinkable to call it a once-in-a-lifetime opportunity. Each one of these children fully intended to be back in a few years' time, and anyone who tried to point out how very few players actually make it this far would be laughed at.

Nobody in the changing room was laughing at Mr Grace, but no one was really listening either.

"So remember all you've been taught:

space, passing, team work, determination, speed, accuracy…" it sounded like he was calling the register!

"OK, let's get ready!"

The team changed into their freshly laundered kit in silence. Most of them couldn't even look each other in the eye. They started to realize just why butterflies were called butterflies! And the queue for the toilets seemed to go on for ever!

Henry's thoughts were different from any of his team mates. From the moment they had come through the main entrance of the ground and walked along the corridor towards the changing rooms, he had tried to imagine what it must have been like forty years earlier. The walls were covered in large black and white photographs of past players and there was a whole wall devoted to Davey Evans. He and Mr Best might have even used the very bench that Henry was now sitting on.

And who knows, the boots in his bag might well have stood on this very floor all those years ago too. Henry reached into his bag to take them out. They must have moved because they weren't under his shorts where he had left them...

Ah! There they were! To his surprise there was a card on top of them. He took it out...

Happy birthday, son! Good luck in the game! Surprise, surprise! I sneaked into your bag this morning and took those old boots out...

Henry froze!

...I've given them back to old Bestie – you won't be needing them now! Happy birthday, love from Dad.

Henry looked into his bag. Inside were the very pair of football boots he had asked for – brand new, polished black with three white stripes stitched into the sides.

This was the worst possible thing that could have happened! It was an absolute disaster!

CHAPTER 24

"Nice boots!" said Alan. "Bet they were a birthday present!"

Henry had no reply.

"OK, team," called Mr Grace. "Off we go then! Come on, Henry, put those boots on; you're going to have to get them dirty sooner or later!"

Henry looked up at his team mates. What could he say to them? They were counting on him to play a blinder. He was meant to be their star player. "Our secret weapon", Mr Grace had called him. How could he tell them that the secret weapon was really those old boots and that without them he was ... well, Banana Feet?

Henry put on his new boots. He had no choice. They were as stiff as wood and they felt very cold. His feet did not tingle.

...And welcome to Highfield Rovers. This glorious stadium has witnessed hundreds of passionate encounters over the years, but few could have matched this for sheer drama. Twenty-two talented hopefuls will be stepping out on the very same turf that their heroes play on each Saturday ... and here they come! Just listen to the crowd roar!

Henry was in a daze. He could hear his name being chanted by countless voices. He knew that his parents and most of his family were watching. And he knew what they were going to see. The very thought made him feel sick. He looked around at the enormous stands that surrounded the pitch. The waving flags and scarves made it look like they were actually moving. What am I doing here? he thought.

"Good luck, Henry!" came a voice from the touchline. It was Mr Best. He was holding the black leather boot-bag in one hand and giving a thumbs-up sign with the other. "You can do it, lad!"

Henry managed a half smile. For one brief moment he thought about running across to him, snatching the bag and swapping boots there and then. But it was out of the question.

So the game gets underway with St John's attacking the goal to our right. They really do look like a powerful side – many of these lads wouldn't look out of place here on a Saturday afternoon!

Henry found himself rooted to the spot. The old boots seemed to react to the kick-off whistle like a sprinter does to a starting pistol. But these new boots did nothing.

St John's, now, on the attack. The ball is played through the middle and Davis, the Holly Park wonder boy, steps up to cut out the pass. Or rather he tries to as the ball slips through his legs and finds its way to the feet of MacDonald, the St John's centre forward. He has a clear shot on goal and shoots. It's there! St John's have an early lead!

"Wake up, Superstar! This is a cup final, not an infant choir rehearsal!" Terry bellowed at Henry as the ball was returned to the centre.

...St John's are certainly dominating the first half. They've struck the post twice and if it wasn't for some heroic goal-keeping by Gary Banks then the game might well have been lost already. There goes the half-time whistle with St John's leading one–nil and Holly Park yet to mount a serious attack.

As the teams left the field Henry didn't dare

look up. He was afraid of catching his father's eye.

"Come on, lad! Keep your chin up!" It was Mr Best. Henry couldn't help himself. He rushed up to him.

"Let me have the boots back!" he pleaded. "Let me have Davey Evans's old boots again! Please!"

Mr Best smiled at Henry. For a second it looked like he was going to cry. "I don't have them," he replied. "I've finally put them where they belong."

"What do you mean?"

"I've handed them over to the club. That's where they're meant to be. Right now they're probably locked away in an office somewhere."

"But I need them!"

"You don't, lad," said Mr Best. "Believe me, you don't." He put his arm around Henry's shoulder. "I know football, lad. You've got it in you!"

"But the boots made me play so well—"

"No. The boots made you believe in yourself, lad. It's you who played well."

Henry found it hard to accept what the caretaker had said. But then he wasn't just a caretaker like Mr Grace was just a teacher. He was a *real* footballer. So he should know.

CHAPTER 25

"If you don't liven your ideas up soon then you're being substituted!" Terry whispered into Henry's ear as the teams came out for the second half. "I've asked Mr Grace and he's giving you five minutes to prove yourself!"

 So the second half gets underway and St John's start the way they finished the first half – on all-out attack.

Henry stood alongside the opposition's centre forward. He was enormous. The ball came to his feet and he turned briskly, brushing Henry aside as if he were made of paper...

...Davis is on the floor. This is certainly not the same player who dominated Winterton so convincingly! But hold on! He's up and charging towards MacDonald. With one swift challenge he scoops the ball away and the attack breaks down. Now that's more like it!

Gradually Henry felt his confidence returning. But St John's were a strong team and time was running out!

St John's have a corner. It comes across and is well punched out by Banks. Davis has the ball now and turns. Immediately two large St John's defenders converge on him. But Davis chips the ball high over their heads and charges right between them. They're stranded and Davis is clear on goal. This is more like it as the Holly Park supporters suddenly find their voices! Davis is on the edge of the box, he lets fly with a terrific shot! Goal! It's the equalizer!

Henry felt taller and stronger than he had ever felt before. He emerged from the pile of relieved team mates and decided to do something he had wanted to do for years...

"Hey, Terry!" he called. "Isn't it time you livened *your* ideas up, Mr Banana Mouth?"

Terry didn't have an answer.

...What a final this has turned into! End-to-end stuff – near misses in both goal mouths. It's anybody's game. Such a delight to watch!

Henry's return to form affected the whole team. They were passing and moving with much more confidence. But St John's were still difficult to break down.

As we move into the last few minutes, the ball is pumped high into the St John's half and is only half-cleared. It lands at the feet of the on-running Davis — surely he's not going to shoot from this far out! He does! It lofts over the keeper and towards the net. Hold on – a defender charges back and dives at the ball. He manages to get a hand to it and pushes it wide. It's a clear penalty to Holly Park with no more than a minute left!

Terry was the regular penalty taker. Everybody knew that. The captain took the ball and walked towards the spot. A hush descended on the stadium.

Suddenly Henry caught sight of Terry's face. It was full of fear. His hands were shaking as he placed the ball. Henry decided to do something about it.

He trotted over to Terry. "You're going to miss," he said firmly. "Don't take it. Let me."

Normally Terry would have pushed Henry aside and walloped it home. But this was not the normal, fearless playground Terry. Here, with hundreds of pairs of eyes watching him, he was as frightened as a mouse in a trap. "OK," he said, "you take it." And he walked away.

 ...This is quite remarkable! The penalty is now going to be taken by Davis and we are well into stoppage time. He steps back...

All Henry saw were upturned buckets. He smiled and swung his foot.

 GOAL!!!! Davis has done it and the ground erupts!

The final whistle blew immediately and Henry was mobbed like he had never been mobbed before. Soon he was sitting on the shoulders of his team mates. He waved to the crowd with his arms flapping like the wings of a newly formed butterfly.

Henry could see all his family. And his

mum was jumping up and down the most!
What a day!

CHAPTER 26

Henry Davis was a hero!

Later that night, sitting at the foot of Henry's bed, his father said, "We were so proud of you! What will you remember most about today?"

Henry thought. "I don't know. Everything, I suppose," he replied.

His father kissed him goodnight and left. Henry could hear him chanting all the way downstairs.

Henry didn't go off to sleep easily. He wondered what he really would remember most about his eleventh birthday. Was it the goals? Lifting the cup? Finally putting Terry in his place? Hearing a whole football stadium singing Happy Birthday to him? Mrs Thorne running a lap of honour in a specially made school uniform? The invitation from a Highfield Rovers scout to come and train with their youth team?

As he lay in the dark Henry stopped wondering. After the game Mr Best had shaken his hand. "I knew you had it in you!" he said. "I've only seen one other footballer play like that, my lad, and you've worn his boots!"

"He must have been very small," Henry replied.

"Those were his boots when he was your age, lad. His mother gave them to me after the accident. 'A little something to remember him by,' she said. I've kept them all these years, but I don't need them any more. If I want to remember the great Davey Evans, all I have to do is look at you!"

"That's what I'll remember most," Henry said to himself and gently went off to sleep.

Author's Note

I love football – I always have. My attic is full of old copies of *Roy of the Rovers* and *The Scorcher*, (Billy's Boots was my favourite). Just like Henry, a large chunk of my childhood was spent perfecting my skills in the garden. Only one thing prevented me from fulfilling my ambition to play for Arsenal – I was useless! No matter how many pairs of boots I tried on – it made no difference.

I was born in 1958, a few weeks after the tragic air crash in Munich that destroyed one of the greatest teams ever – Manchester United's legendary Busby Babes. This story is a tribute to the memory of the greatest of them all, Duncan Edwards; a prodigious talent that was so cruelly extinguished. May his memory live on in the ambitions of every aspiring soccer superstar.